P O C

OTHER BOOKS BY STUART ROSS

A Sparrow Came Down Resplendent (Wolsak and Wynn, 2016)

Sonnets, w/ Richard Huttel (serif of nottingham editions, 2016)

A Hamburger in a Gallery (DC Books, 2015)

Further Confessions of a Small-Press Racketeer (Anvil Press, 2015)

In In My Dreams (BookThug, 2014)

A Pretty Good Year (Nose in Book Publishing, 2014)

Nice Haircut, Fiddlehead (Puddles of Sky Press, 2014)

Our Days in Vaudeville (Mansfield Press, 2013)

You Exist. Details Follow. (Anvil Press, 2012)

Snowball, Dragonfly, Jew (ECW Press, 2011)

I Have Come to Talk About Manners (Apt. 9 Press, 2010)

Buying Cigarettes for the Dog (Freehand Books, 2009)

Dead Cars in Managua (DC Books, 2008)

I Cut My Finger (Anvil Press, 2007)

Confessions of a Small-Press Racketeer (Anvil Press, 2005)

Hey, Crumbling Balcony! Poems New & Selected (ECW Press, 2003)

Razovsky at Peace (ECW Press, 2001)

Farmer Gloomy's New Hybrid (ECW Press, 1999)

Henry Kafka & Other Stories (The Mercury Press, 1997)

The Inspiration Cha-Cha (ECW Press, 1996)

The Mud Game, w/ Gary Barwin (The Mercury Press, 1995)

The Pig Sleeps, w/ Mark Laba (Contra Mundo Books, 1993)

POCKETS

a novel

by Stuart Ross

MISFIT

Published by ECW Press
665 Gerrard Street East, Toronto, ON M4M 1Y2
416-694-3348 / info@ecwpress.com

LIBRARY AND ARCHIVES CANADA
CATALOGUING IN PUBLICATION

Ross, Stuart, author
Pockets : a novel / by Stuart Ross.

Issued in print and electronic formats.
ISBN 978-1-77041-383-2 (softcover)
ISBN 978-1-77305-088-1 (PDF)
ISBN 978-1-77305-089-8 (EPUB)

I. Title.

PS8585.O841P63 2017   C813'.54   C2017-903741-2
C2017-903742-0

Editor for the press:
Michael Holmes /
M I S F I T   a misFit book

Cover illustration and design:
Catrina Longmuir
Type: Rachel Ironstone

The publication of *Pockets* has been generously supported by the Canada Council for the Arts, which last year invested $153 million to bring the arts to Canadians throughout the country, and by the Government of Canada through the Canada Book Fund. *Nous remercions le Conseil des arts du Canada de son soutien. L'an dernier, le Conseil a investi 153 millions de dollars pour mettre de l'art dans la vie des Canadiennes et des Canadiens de tout le pays. Ce livre est financé en partie par le gouvernement du Canada.* We also acknowledge the support of the Ontario Arts Council (OAC), an agency of the Government of Ontario, which last year funded 1,737 individual artists and 1,095 organizations in 223 communities across Ontario for a total of $52.1 million, and the contribution of the Government of Ontario through the Ontario Book Publishing Tax Credit and the Ontario Media Development Corporation.

Ontario
Ontario Media Development Corporation

ONTARIO ARTS COUNCIL
CONSEIL DES ARTS DE L'ONTARIO
an Ontario government agency
un organisme du gouvernement de l'Ontario

Printed and bound in Canada
Coach House Printing   5   4   3   2   1

"He had a choice of being the wave that rolls onto the shore or the one that rolls into the sea."

Toby MacLennan,
1 Walked out of 2 and Forgot It

"No. No, I was not alone."

John Lavery,
Sandra Beck

POCKETS

I looked out my bedroom window and saw my brother floating over the weeping willows. His feet fluttered, as if he were wearing flippers. His arms trailed at his sides, his fingertips pointing back to where he had just come from. Where he had just come from now looked like a hovering oil slick, glittering with traces of the moon's pale light.

The houses crouched in their yards, amid the damp grass, and they breathed almost silently. Every so often one twitched or shuddered. Rain streaked down their windows. The tip of an evergreen was tilted by the wind, but it pushed back, straightening itself until it pointed toward the thick clouds.

A comet whipped through the night sky. The next comet waited its turn. And still more after that one, more and more comets. There was some jostling in the line, a bit of shoving, and then calm.

I stood in my bedroom, at the foot of my unmade bed. I turned on a lamp and my shadow was thrown across the floor. With effort, it pulled itself to its feet and lurched toward the window. The phone rang once and then whoever it was hung up.

I reached into the bottom of my pants pockets, grasped the seams, and pulled the pockets out till they looked like dog ears flopping against my thighs. They were empty. I counted to eighteen, and stuffed them back into my pants. Then I scooped up palmfuls of my own shadow from the floor and filled my pockets with them.

Pants are trousers. Trousers are slacks. Shirts are blouses. Socks are stockings. That summer, I dug for clams while wearing clam-diggers. Or maybe I dug for trilobites. Was it trilobites?

Morning arrived. The house was silent. It didn't move. I looked out the window. My brother stood in the backyard, beside the red-brick barbecue our father had built. He reached forward and his hand grew immense. He wrapped his enormous fingers around the house and crammed it into his pocket. I turned on my lamp, and everything disappeared.

The door to my parents' bedroom was shut. Gently, I pushed it open and peeked in. The television threw a glow onto their bed. They lay side by side, my mother and father, completely still. I heard the voice of Deborah Kerr in *The Innocents*. It was, therefore, sometime after 1961. I slipped out of the house, into my car, and drove to the cemetery. I reached into my pockets, took out some small rocks, and placed them on the headstone my parents shared.

The Hebrew alphabet has twenty-two letters. The Hebrew school I attended was located in the basement of the synagogue near our house. The teacher called me by my Hebrew name — Zalman. It takes four Hebrew letters to spell Zalman. There are four stages involved in something or other to do with the Kabbalah. It is marvellous how everything is connected.

On Easter Island, there are heads made of stone. Eight hundred and eighty-seven of them. The men who carved them rubbed the gigantic heads with pumice when they were finished. I liked to sit at my piano and play *Trois Gymnopédies*. Who doesn't? Erik Satie, who composed it, cleaned his skin with a pumice stone, one square inch at a time.

The boy next door and I sat under the wooden porch in his backyard, examining the small grey stones, one at a time, rolling them in our fingers, looking for trilobite fossils. His shiny black yarmulke fell off, and he put it back on over his shiny black hair, then pushed the bobby pin into place. This was called archaeology.

I crouched inside the snow fort. I ate some ice. The sounds from outside were muffled. I ate some more ice. The ice made crunching noises as I chewed it. The world outside was destroyed when we collided with another planet. I floated through space in my silent snow fort. When I looked out the door, I saw stars, stars, stars against the endless black nothingness.

I peered through my living room window at the house across the street and into their living room window. I could see my friend Stevie. He reached down and pulled out his pants pockets. Coins fell out, and raisins. A baseball glove and a twisted menorah. Newts scampered down his legs, and goldfish drifted into the air, as if the living room were filled with water. Stevie pushed his pockets back into his pants, wiped the back of one hand across his nostrils, and disappeared from my view. Soon his front door opened. He appeared on the porch. Then he was on the roof. Then he stepped out of his open garage. He walked away down our street, down Pannahill Road. The street rolled up after him, revealing a dark ravine beneath.

I looked at my wristwatch in disbelief. "Why don't you believe me?" it asked.

As I sat cross-legged on the floor of my parents' bedroom at lunchtime watching *The Flintstones* on television, I felt a tickle on the knuckles of my right hand. It was a daddy-long-legs. Or maybe it was the 1955 movie *Daddy Long Legs*, starring Fred Astaire as Jervis Pendleton III and Leslie Caron as Julie Andre. Whichever it was, it scurried across the back of my hand and vanished.

On the sidewalk, two men faced each other. One man said, "Mister, can you spare a quarter?" The other man pulled his empty pockets out of his slacks, as if to say, "Admire the fine material."

I pedalled my new red bicycle to the end of the block. I looked back at our house. My brother stood at the foot of the driveway watching me. He wore a white T-shirt and blue jeans. I was not allowed to ride any farther than the stop sign. I looked at the grey-and-yellow triplexes a block away. Marky lived in one. I rode past the stop sign and up, up, toward the triplexes. I wobbled from side to side on my red bicycle. My brother snitched. The slam of my father's footsteps as he strode after me along Pannahill Road was like a series of meteors hitting the earth. I stood with Marky looking at my new bicycle, and soon my father's shadow fell over us. His large thumb came down and squashed me into the concrete. Marky examined the smudge on the driveway in front of the triplex he lived in.

Back on earth, some people didn't have houses. Meanwhile, some houses didn't have people.

My father was handy. In the basement, next to the furnace, he had a workshop full of tools and pieces of wood and metal. Also, he banged nails into walls and hung paintings on them. Once, he missed the nail and struck his thumb with the hammer. When my friends came over, they always asked to look at his cleft thumb.

In the black-and-white photo taken ten years before I was born, my father and mother look like movie stars. They stand in a field, wind whispering through their hair. The photo whispered in my ear, "See how they smile. See their eyes shine. They have no worries yet, your parents."

In the ravine behind my school, I walked along the snow-covered path. I watched my breath turn into clouds. I could hear my own breathing. My boots squeaked on the ground. A thing caught my eye and I knelt. I brushed away some snow with my mittened hand. The face of a frozen squirrel was revealed. It looked into my eyes.

My father followed the ambulance that carried my brother to the hospital. The red lights on top of the ambulance flashed in his chest. Crisp brown leaves drifted from the trees and swirled in the streets. He arrived soon after the ambulance. Later that night, I sat on the foot of his bed. He lay on top of the covers, his clothes rumpled, his hair rumpled, red lights flashing in his chest. He rubbed his dark eyes. "I tried to save him," he said.

A boll weevil curled up into a tiny grey ball on the grey curb. It rocked slightly in the warm breeze. A 1966 blue Ford station wagon rolled by. Neither the boll weevil nor the station wagon was aware of the other. A sprinkling of rain began to fall. Soon the entire road looked like it was covered by shadow.

My mother. Her lips touched my forehead. She walked out the front door. A winter draft swept across the floor toward me and bowled me over. I heard her start her car. My grandfather's voice from downstairs. He called her name. I drifted along the hardwood floor. He called her name again. On the television, a president got shot in the head.

I closed my bedroom door and stood on my bed. I rolled up an *Archie* comic and held it to my mouth like a microphone. I opened my mouth. I thought of Herman's Hermits and "Mrs. Brown You've Got a Lovely Daughter." I thought of Gerry and the Pacemakers and "I Like It." I took a breath. Soon I would hear my voice. I wondered what it would sound like.

In our basement was an old fridge. The noise it made was louder than the stuttering hum of the new fridge upstairs in our kitchen. It was white with a silver handle. It contained a turkey. The turkey had presented itself to my father as a reward for my father's success in bowling. My father took three or four long strides. The ball left his hands. The sound of the ball rolling down the lane is the sound of me not remembering what that sound sounded like.

The phone rang. It hung on the kitchen wall and rang. Its dangling curled cord swayed slightly. We all sat at the dinner table and watched it ring. A green bowl of corn niblets on the counter watched it ring, too. It rang eight times and then it stopped.

The girl next door had never heard of the Beatles. I laughed. She laughed, too. Her name was Karen. She showed me her *Cowsills* comic book, and her mother gave us peanut-butter sandwiches and milk in glasses that had once held yahrzeit candles. I looked out their kitchen window and saw my own house. My grandfather was standing on the roof beside his treadle-operated sewing machine. He was born in Poland, and he clenched a piece of thread between his teeth.

Spools of black, brown, and grey thread emerged from the clouds, unravelling as they sailed down toward earth. Earth, meanwhile, braced itself.

My mother lay in the hospital bed. The nurse injected a needle into her thigh. She asked me to hold a piece of cotton hard against the spot where the needle had entered, then she left the room, and I was alone with my mother. My hand trembled. I wasn't sure whether my mother was awake. Her television was on. It was news. It was a trial. I stood there pressing the piece of cotton against my mother's thigh. Days passed. I placed a rock on her headstone. A spool landed beside my feet.

I ran down the empty street. I passed through the yellow glow of street lamp after street lamp. My running shoes slapped the pavement. Thunder rumbled in the distance.

The Angel of Death flew out of our Haggadah and slew me with a sword. On Passover, my mother and father and brother and grandfather opened the Haggadah to read and pray and sing, and they saw the woodcut image of me skewered on the sword. "I thought he was up in his room," my father said.

When I woke up, I was surprised to find myself swimming through the air, my skin cool and damp from a light drizzle. Beneath me was an enormous weeping willow. I passed the window of a house, where a small lamp threw light on the face of a boy lying in his bed, looking across the room and out the window. Just before he left my field of vision, I recognized the boy as me, peering out the window at his brother drifting by.

Marky and I performed *The Marriage of Figaro* in the garage of my house. This consisted of us standing on the concrete floor singing, "Figaro, Figaro, Figaro," over and over again. Then we told some jokes and talked in funny voices. For his ventriloquism demonstration, Marky used a stuffed toy animal that my dog, Rufus, had humped. The garage door was closed and the performance was illuminated by a single light bulb hanging from the ceiling. All the corners of the garage were shrouded in shadows and probably filled with spiders. The five audience members sat on car tires and on cardboard boxes filled with shingles. It smelled like oil in there, or maybe gasoline. Admission to our show was only five cents, and the value was excellent. One of the jokes was: "What do ghosts eat for breakfast?" The answer was: "Evaporated milk and ghost toast."

I stood in the ninth-floor hallway of my grandparents' apartment building. I opened the door marked "GARBAGE" and stepped into the tiny garbage room. It smelled like garbage. I opened the garbage chute and peered down. It smelled like garbage. The building turned upside down and I landed on the ceiling.

Tiny spiders were lowering themselves from my parents' ceiling. They were all over the place. My mother said they came out of the curtains. The curtains depicted scenes from Venice. Canals and gondoliers. I ran from the room, brushing at my hair frantically to knock any spiders away. Those spiders were so tiny. I could feel them in my hair for the rest of the day.

Marky did not like the books about the boy detectives. "Look, this is a good one," I said. "This is a good one, too, I like this one." There were thousands of them and they were all good. You got to know everybody. Frank and Joe Hardy. Chet Morton. Fenton Hardy. Aunt Gertrude. Iola Morton, and Biff Hooper. Also Phil Cohen. I peered at the page in disbelief. There was a Phil Cohen.

Stevie was on his lawn, cutting grass with hedge clippers. "Look," he said, "I'm cutting the grass!" I reached in to help clear away some of the cut grass. The tip of my right index finger got snipped off. Stevie ran away. In the hospital, they put a rubber thing that looked like a nipple over my finger. My parents had to apply Mercurochrome four times a day. It stained my finger red. I refused to go to school with a nipple-finger.

Music came out of the radio on the kitchen table. The song was very repetitive. The house was empty. The telephone was silent. A bird hit the living room window.

I pulled out my pockets to prove that I had nothing in my pockets. He pushed me on the grass and laughed and bicycled away. I got up and brushed the dirt and blades of grass off my pants. Later I watched *Thumbelina* at the Willow Theatre. Coke travelled up through a red-and-white-striped straw, into my mouth.

Tadpoles swimming in circles through murky water in a bowl on my dresser. Dust floating in the beams of sunlight gushing in through the window. Cartoon frogs with hats and canes singing, "Give my regards to Broadway." This is how we lived in those days.

On the floor of my brother's bedroom, which years earlier had been my bedroom, until I moved out and my brother moved back in, lay bits of tape, torn plastic pouches, a damp towel, a plastic syringe: the detritus of his collapse and the paramedics' efforts. I went back into my father's bedroom. He was asleep. It was four-thirty in the morning. A photo of my mother, before she became sick, stood on the nightstand beside him. A movie starring Jean-Claude Van Damme was on the TV. When my father woke up, it would be time to choose a casket for the funeral that afternoon. I wandered to the sunken living room, wanting to sit at my old piano and see if I remembered Erik Satie. But the living room was filled with water, reaching up the piano's legs. I saw flashes of eels and Chinese goldfish beneath the water's dark surface. A crocodile lounged on the steps leading down. I went into the dining room, sat at the table, and slowly spun the lazy Susan until the sun came up and the windows shattered.

A noise from my closet. I turned on my lamp. I was in a room I didn't recognize. When I turned my lamp off, then on again, I was back in my own room. My shadow thrown against the wall looked like Danny Kaye in a scene from *The Man from the Diners' Club*.

Marky and I sat cross-legged on the hardwood floor of his living room, in front of the stereo. A Jewish-soup smell came from the kitchen. He lowered the stylus onto the vinyl and it bounced a moment, then played a song by Randy Newman, "Lonely at the Top." I met Randy Newman backstage at his concert at Convocation Hall. We both had big noses, glasses, pot-bellies, and curly grey hair. Randy Newman squinted at me and said, "It's like I'm looking at myself twenty years ago." I asked Marky to play "Simon Smith and the Amazing Dancing Bear" again.

I looked out my bedroom window. My brother swam past once more through the sky. "I told you I could do this," he said. I climbed into the window frame to watch him through the screen as he got farther away, until the speck of him disappeared into a dark cloud. I opened my fist and in my palm I discovered a tiny ambulance, its red lights flashing.

If a ghost floats in through your window in the middle of the night, is it impolite to ask whose ghost it is?

My father and mother were in the front seat of the Ford station wagon, facing out the front window, and my brother and I were in the small back seat at the rear of the wagon, facing out the back window. We were on the highway. When a car pulled up behind the station wagon, so close that we could see the driver's face, my brother and I waved. If the driver waved back, we got one point.

The phone rang. Nobody was home. The lamps were off, and a rolled-up newspaper shivered on the porch. The president's head was a puddle, a mess. After several rings, the phone answered. There was a phone on the other end.

Across the border, in Vineland, New Jersey, I chased fireflies around on my aunt's lawn and tried to put them in a jar with holes punched into the tin lid. I looked at them more closely and saw they were tiny ambulances with their lights flashing. My aunt came out to call me for dinner and found me crammed into the jar instead, my curly hair poking up through the breathing holes. "After we eat," she said, lifting up the jar that held me, "we'll go to the casino. I go to the casino every Saturday."

A small animal woke to find itself covered in snow. It could not move, could not even shiver, although its entire body felt cold. Its mother used to say, *Stay in and play today. It's bitterly cold outside.* It wondered what sort of animal it was, then became aware of its large bushy tail. All around it lay the detritus of its collapse.

A boy on the street looked at me as we passed each other. We were both wearing blue shorts and a Batman T-shirt. We watched each other as we slowly walked backwards. We forgot who was who.

I knelt in front of a piece of paper on the linoleum kitchen floor. I clutched a pencil. I drew a lady whose breasts pointed out like they were reaching for something. One of her breasts was on top of the other. I put nipple dots at the tip of each breast. My brother walked into the kitchen and opened the fridge. I covered my drawing with both hands.

I sat on the floor eating a bowl of potato chips and drinking Coke from a green plastic tumbler. My grandmother was in the kitchen frying up chicken fat with chicken skin and onions. My grandfather was behind me, sitting on his enormous recliner. The television was on. The show was *Lawrence Welk*. A lady with short black hair and a short black dress with sparkles on it was dancing. "She's a knockout," my grandfather said. I watched the lady for a while. It was the first time I'd heard my grandfather not complain.

I was looking for Stevie. It was getting dark. I checked behind a stack of tires in his garage; in the bushes in front of his house; in my own backyard, behind the red-brick barbecue my father built; inside the dented garbage cans at the side of my neighbours' house. "Stevie, come out!" I yelled. "The game is over! I have to go eat supper!" Then a car pulled up and he stepped out. He was an adult now and carried a briefcase. The weight of my own body had become considerable. I reached a hand to my face and found a short rough beard. We stood before each other and squinted. Soon a woman's voice rang through the dusk. "Stevie! Dinner!"

Dinner, supper. Pants, slacks. Shirt, blouse. Pop, soda, cola. Couch, chesterfield, sofa, divan. And then Phil Cohen.

A little boy from down the street threw a firecracker at me. It was a small firecracker. A ladyfinger. His sister, who was older, came over and grabbed his arm. "I'm sorry, he shouldn't do that," she said, and she led him away. She had a TV star on her shirt.

On the basement steps, on a piece of paper, I drew a guy getting shot by an arrow. Blood spurted out of his chest and gradually filled up the whole piece of paper.

My mother told me the large tree in our backyard was called a "weeping willow." It drooped toward the lawn like it was sad. It was sad because the president got shot in the head.

I stood at my bedroom window, looking out into the stars and at the moon, so small, drifting across the black sky. The house was silent. My room was dark. My pyjamas were covered in squirrels. The thing I thought was the moon was not the moon, after all. It was a snow fort. I huddled inside it, chewing ice.

It was impossible, in a ravine, to not walk through spiderwebs. You got web on your face, and spiders, and dead flying insects. You screamed and clawed your fingernails across your face. You spat. You tugged at your hair. Meanwhile, just a few metres from you, there might have been a body of some person lying there amid the trees, under the mulch, in a shallow grave, decomposing.

The president got shot in the head. The guy at the gas station near our house got shot in the stomach. In the United States people got shot in the head, and in Canada they got shot in the stomach. My cousin married a guy who heard I liked peanuts, so he brought me a bag of them every time.

A square of sky obliterated by dark clouds. Then: my brother. Then: a square of sky obliterated by dark clouds.

I told Marky about a book I was reading. It was the story of a seal named Oscar who battled Nazi U-boats. In both our cases, Marky's and mine, Nazis killed lots of members of our families, but before we were ever born. Some seals balanced beach balls on their noses and some took on the Nazis.

My father stood beside his car in the driveway. He reached into his pockets and turned them inside out. Then he made a funny face. This was his Red Skelton impersonation. He drove me to the park and stood around smoking cigarettes while I played on the monkey bars. Then I stood around smoking while he played on the monkey bars. Soon it was time to go home for supper.

The name of the road my house was on was Pannahill Road. Nobody was named Pannahill. There isn't a country called Pannahill. A pannahill is not a thing.

The headstone stood in front of me. It wore rocks on its head. It watched me shift from foot to foot in the cold, watched me jam my hands deep in my pockets. It saw my lips moving and heard sounds come out, but it didn't understand language. My eyes were red and filled with tears. The headstone just stood there, waiting for me to leave: *It's the same thing every time. He just comes up here and stands right in front of me and his eyes turn red and sounds issue from his mouth. Where are the rocks on his head? Where are the words carved into his chest?*

I opened my eyes in the dark. The curtains were open. I was just in time to see a pair of feet flutter slowly beyond the left side of the window frame, then disappear.

My father's big strides covered the length of the hospital corridors in just seconds. He hadn't slept in several days. He was waiting for my mother to wake up. Sometimes I sat beside her and read a book. Sometimes I went to the cafeteria and ate french fries. The ketchup packets looked up at me. I plunged them into my pockets.

In the synagogue, after Saturday-morning service, all the old men went to the adjoining room, where they held chickpeas on paper napkins in the palms of their hands. The women sipped tea from foam cups. We, the children, prayed that it would all soon be over. My friend Kenny's uncle Norm shook everybody's hands. When I became old, I would eat chickpeas.

My father moved out of our house for three weeks. Then he moved back in. I phoned Marky. This had not happened at his home. But his father brought him a newt in a glass bowl. At night, when Marky was sleeping, the newt grew giant and red and pounded through the streets. It found the children who had bullied Marky, ripped them from their beds, and pulled their heads off. In the morning, it was in its bowl, cute and green again.

The president who got shot in the head was moved to the house at the corner of Pannahill Road. Sometimes when we walked by, we saw him peek out from between the curtains. His head looked like it was wrapped in a turban. When he saw us see him, he pulled the curtains closed and the house looked casual again, like it was just standing there on the corner watching some birds in the trees, like nothing much was happening.

Karen, the girl next door, was playing badminton with her friend. I watched through our window. They had set up a net in Karen's backyard. Her friend wore a T-shirt with a TV star on it. The birdie sailed way up into the air, seemed to float on the breeze, before falling back down to earth. It didn't care that she hadn't heard of the Beatles.

Houses and trees and buildings and people were whipping by. Marky and I were in the back seat of his father's red Pontiac Tempest. We each had a big book on our laps and on the big book a sheet of white paper. The books were there so our pencils didn't poke through the paper and wreck our drawings. Marky's father drove the car off the edge of the road, and we plunged into a ravine. This was the ravine where Marky and I sometimes caught frogs. The car landed on its side. Trees grew right up through the windows. Marky's father told us stories about being a cook on a navy ship. Sometimes the sailors, even though they were tough, got so seasick that they threw up their dinners right out the windows. After two hundred years passed, a helicopter lowered a ladder and we climbed to safety. Marky's father pointed: "Look, you can see the ship I worked on right over there." We followed his finger, but all we saw was the Kresge's department store and a man running out of it waving a gun in his left hand.

I was alone. It was dark. I turned on a lamp and my shadow leapt across the floor. I leapt after it.

Stevie came over for lunch. My mother made us noodle soup and cheese sandwiches on challah. We sat at the kitchen table and ate. Stevie spit out his first spoonful of the soup. "This isn't how *my* mother makes it!" he shouted. He found a spade and dug a large rectangular hole in the kitchen floor. He filled it with water from our tap and jumped in for a swim. He swam around and around, like a goldfish. My mother and I pretended not to notice him as we finished our lunch.

At summer camp, they made me swim in my pyjamas. I swam ten lengths between the pier and an orange buoy. Then they gave me a certificate saying I could swim while I was at camp because I had successfully swum in my pyjamas. I didn't swim again after that.

I woke up in the dark. It was winter and my bedroom window was closed. I heard a faint tapping on it. My brother was floating there, his face to the window, his fingertips hitting the glass. I pushed the covers aside and walked to the window. I tried to turn the crank that opened it, but my hand kept slipping. "I want to talk to you, too," I told my brother. But I couldn't get hold of the crank. Soon a thin layer of snow covered my trembling window.

I went to another country and collected rocks to place on the headstones. I found the rocks in various locations: beaches, sidewalks, gardens, forests. Then I came home.

I was driving a car, but I can't remember if I was a child or an adult. I reached a hand to my face. It was rough, unshaven. I was an adult. But when I looked at the passenger seat, there was an *Archie* comic lying on it. I pulled the car over to the side of the road and stepped out. I was wearing a Batman T-shirt. Another man walked by wearing a Batman T-shirt. We stood in front of each other. We almost opened our mouths but then decided not to. We reached into our pockets and pulled out the linings. From mine dropped a small plastic soldier, orange. From his dropped an ad torn from a comic book, featuring a pair of X-ray glasses. We forgot who was who.

Then, out of the sky, my mother's hand reached down. With her fingertips, she brushed my hair off my forehead, away from my eyes. I looked far beyond the paved roads and also the houses, with all the activity taking place inside them, all the people and televisions and dogs and lamps in every room, and I saw paths leading into woods, and soon the paths stopped, they just stopped, and the vegetation became too dense for me to go any farther, but I knew things were happening within that denseness. I shoved my hands into my pockets and walked into the clouds.

ACKNOWLEDGEMENTS

Without Toby MacLennan's sublime novel *1 Walked out of 2 and Forgot It* (Something Else Press, 1972), which blew my teenage mind, *Pockets* would not exist. A bonus is that four decades after I first read her book, we embarked on a lovely correspondence. I am grateful to — and in awe of — my friend and collaborator Catrina Longmuir for her care in creating the perfect cover for this book. Laurie Siblock provided valuable feedback and cheerleading for this project. I am grateful again to the busy gang at ECW, particularly editor Michael Holmes, who is always supportive of my wiggy projects, copy editor Laura Pastore, who did a damn good job, and Rachel Ironstone, sharp proofreader and text designer. My friends Dag Straumsvåg, in Trondheim, and Sarah Moses, in Buenos Aires, offered excellent close readings and encouragement. Gratitude, too, to my generous Patreon supporters. And thanks, as always, to those who buy my books, those who borrow them from public libraries, and those who send kind notes to me at razovsky@gmail.com.

ABOUT STUART ROSS

Stuart Ross is a writer, editor, teacher, and small press activist living in Cobourg, Ontario. He is the author of twenty books of poetry, fiction, and essays. His novel *Snowball, Dragonfly, Jew* (ECW Press, 2011) was the 2012 co-winner of the Mona Elaine Adilman Award for Fiction on a Jewish Theme, and in 2013 his poetry collection *You Exist. Details Follow.* (Anvil Press, 2012) took the only prize awarded to a work by an Anglophone writer by l'Académie de la vie littéraire au tournant du 21ême siècle. Stuart has read and taught workshops across the country, and was the 2010 Writer-in-Residence at Queen's University. He is at work on about a dozen different poetry, non-fiction, and fiction manuscripts.

Get the eBook FREE!

At ECW Press, we want you to enjoy this book in whatever format you like, whenever you like. Leave your print book at home and take the eBook to go! Purchase the print edition and receive the eBook free. Just send an e-mail to ebook@ecwpress.com and include:

- the book title
- the name of the store where you purchased it
- your receipt number
- your preference of file type: PDF or ePub?

A real person will respond to your e-mail with your eBook attached. Thank you for supporting an independently owned Canadian publisher with your purchase!